Humphrey's
Mixed-Up Magic Trick

Look for all of
HUMPHREY'S TINY TALES

Humphrey's
Mixed-Up Magic Trick

Betty G. Birney

illustrated by **Priscilla Burris**

G. P. PUTNAM'S SONS

To a magical couple,
Caroline and Walshe
—B.B.

For Kathy & Marc McNeely
and Pam & Dave Woods
—P.B.

G. P. Putnam's Sons
an imprint of Penguin Random House LLC
375 Hudson Street, New York, NY 10014

Text copyright © 2016 by Betty G. Birney.
Illustrations copyright © 2016 by Priscilla Burris.

G. P. Putnam's Sons is a registered trademark of Penguin Random House LLC.

Library of Congress Cataloging-in-Publication Data
Names: Birney, Betty G., author. | Burris, Priscilla, illustrator.
Title: Humphrey's mixed-up magic trick / Betty G. Birney ; illustrated by Priscilla Burris.
Description: New York, NY : G. P. Putnam's Sons, [2016] | Series: Humphrey's tiny tales ; 5
Summary: "The students of Room 26 are doing reports about the jobs they want to have when they grow up—and Humphrey the classroom pet hamster helps aspiring magician Miranda show the class about her own dream job"—Provided by publisher.
Identifiers: LCCN 2015029014 | ISBN 9780399172304 (hardback) | ISBN 9780147514615 (paperback)
Subjects: | CYAC: Hamsters—Fiction. | Schools—Fiction. | Occupations—Fiction. | Magicians—Fiction. | Magic tricks—Fiction. | BISAC: JUVENILE FICTION / Readers / Chapter Books. | JUVENILE FICTION / Animals / Mice, Hamsters, Guinea Pigs, etc. | JUVENILE FICTION / Imagination & Play.
Classification: LCC PZ7.B5229 Hs 2016 | DDC [Fic]—dc23
LC record available at http://lccn.loc.gov/2015029014

Printed in the United States of America.
ISBN 978-0-399-17230-4
1 3 5 7 9 10 8 6 4 2

Design by Ryan Thomann. Text set in ITC Stone Informal Std Medium.

Contents

Homework

I've learned about a lot of things in my job as classroom hamster.

I've learned about reading, writing, math, history and science.

I've also learned about art and music.

Oh, yes, and I've also learned a lot about *homework*.

You see, my classmates work hard in Room 26. But they also work hard outside of Room 26. Our teacher, Mrs. Brisbane, gives them work to do at home.

I don't have to turn in my homework, but I do it anyway.

I work out math problems and learn to spell new words in a little notebook. It's a secret

and I keep it
hidden behind
the mirror in my cage.

But one day, Mrs. Brisbane
gave us a special homework
assignment.

"Class, I want you to choose

a job you think you'd like to do when you grow up," she said.

"Did you say a *job*?" Repeat-It-Please-Richie asked.

"That's right," Mrs. Brisbane replied. "Find out what it takes to be good at that job. Then, next Monday, you'll share what you learned with the class. And I want you to come dressed as a person who does that job."

This assignment caused quite a buzz.

"When I grow up, I'm going to be a soccer player!" Lower-Your-Voice-A.J.  announced. "And you can all cheer for me."

"It depends what team you're on," Garth said.

Sit-Still-Seth leaped out of his seat. "I want to be a doctor and help sick people get well," he said.

"Good for you, Seth!" I squeaked.

5

I know that all he heard was SQUEAK-SQUEAK-SQUEAK, but at least he could tell how much I liked the idea.

The other classroom pet, Og the Frog, agreed.

"BOING-BOING!" he said in his funny, twangy voice.

"*I'm* going to be a teacher, just like Mrs. Brisbane," Stop-Giggling-Gail said.

It was hard to imagine a teacher who giggles as much as Gail does. But her classroom would always be fun.

"I'm going to be a comedian," Kirk said. "Here's a joke: Why did the teacher wear sunglasses in class?"

"I don't know, Kirk. Why?" Mrs. Brisbane asked.

"Because her class was so bright!" Kirk laughed.

Mrs. Brisbane laughed, too. "I'm sure you will be a comedian, Kirk. And you're right—I do have a bright group of students."

Then she turned to the class. "You have a lot of good ideas, so just remember that the report is due Monday," she said. "And come in costume!"

"How are we supposed to know what we'll want to do then?" Richie asked. "I'm not grown up yet."

Mrs. Brisbane smiled. "That's true. You'll probably change your mind a few times before you do grow up. But it's still fun to think about things you'd like to do. Don't you have any ideas?"

Richie thought for a few seconds. "I might be a chef because I like to eat. Or I might be a police officer and put bad guys in jail," he said. "Or I might be an Olympic runner. I'm pretty fast."

I tried to picture Richie if he had all of those jobs. He'd look pretty silly dressed in a police uniform, running down a track, carrying a tray of yummy food.

"Those are all good ideas, Richie," Mrs. Brisbane said. "Just pick *one* for your report."

When the final bell rang, my classmates hurried out of the classroom. I heard Sayeh ask Golden-Miranda what she wanted to do when she grows up.

"I'll tell you later," Miranda answered. "But I don't think anyone else will have the same idea."

She had a funny smile on her face. It made me very curious about what she was thinking.

Once Og and I were alone in Room 26, I jiggled the lock-that-doesn't-lock on my cage. I climbed out and scurried over to his tank.

"Og, I already have a job as a classroom pet. So do you," I told him.

"BOING-BOING-*BOING*!" Og replied.

"But if I couldn't be a classroom pet, could I do another job?" I said.

Og didn't answer. Instead, he dived into the water side of his tank and began to splash.

I ducked out of the way because we hamsters don't like to get wet. Then I scurried back to my cage.

I took out my notebook and pencil and wrote:

JOBS I COULD DO
(Besides Classroom Pet)

I didn't write anything else because I wasn't sure *what* jobs a hamster could do. Of course, instead of being a classroom pet, I could be a child's pet. Many hamsters have that job and their families love them. So I scribbled:

FAMILY PET

I sat and thought some more.

My whiskers wiggled. My tail twitched. But I couldn't think of a single other job for a hamster.

And then I remembered that Mrs. Brisbane's husband once took me to a place called Maycrest Manor. The humans staying there loved to watch me do tricks and run mazes.

They were people who were recovering from being sick or getting hurt. And I have to say, I really cheered them up! So I wrote down:

CHEERING-UP HAMSTER

I thought
some more.

There must
be MANY-MANY-MANY jobs for
a smart and curious hamster
like me.

Sometimes I follow clues to
figure out what problems my
friends are having. So I wrote:

HAMSTER DETECTIVE

And I sometimes spin, leap,
twirl and whirl to entertain my

friends. They really enjoy seeing me roll around the room in my hamster ball or hang from the tippy top of my cage. So I wrote:

HAMSTER ENTERTAINER

I stared at those words for a few minutes. They just didn't seem right.

So I changed it.

HAMSTER ~~ENTERTAINER~~ STAR

I looked at my list and I was soooo proud! Although I never want to leave my job as a classroom pet, it was nice to know that I had choices.

And it was also nice to know that I had a good start on my homework!

Magic-Miranda

The next day, I took a little nap when my classmates were outside for recess. But loud voices near my cage woke me up.

"It is *too* a real job!" That was Golden-Miranda speaking.

Miranda Golden is a favorite friend of mine. I love her golden hair. It reminds me of my nice golden fur.

I like everything about her except for her dog, Clem. He has sharp teeth and very bad breath!

"It's not a job like a firefighter. Or a soccer player!" That was A.J.'s loud voice.

I poked my head out of my bedding.

A.J. was standing in front of Miranda with his arms folded.

"It's the job I'm doing when I grow up," she said.

A.J. shook his head. "Even if it is a job, *girls* don't do it."

"What job?" I squeaked, but I don't think anyone heard me.

Then Speak-Up-Sayeh came over. "Of course women do that job," she said in her soft voice.

"Maybe." A.J. rolled his eyes. "But none of them are famous!"

A.J.'s voice got Pay-Attention-Art's attention.

"A.J.'s right." Art stepped forward. "*None* of them!"

That made Miranda look REALLY-REALLY-REALLY angry.

I hopped out of my bedding and climbed up the side of my cage.

"Mrs. Brisbane! Where are you?" I squeaked at the top of my tiny lungs.

Just then, our teacher rushed over and asked, "Will someone please tell me what you're arguing about?"

A.J. pointed to Miranda. "*She* picked something that's not a real job. And even if it is a real job, girls don't do it."

Miranda pointed at A.J.
"He's *wrong*."

"Calm down, both of you," Mrs. Brisbane said. "What do you want to do, Miranda?"

Miranda glared at A.J. "I'm going to be a magician. I'm going to be a *great* magician. And I really mean it!"

"Of course you do," Mrs. Brisbane said. "That is a real job. There are people who make a living doing magic acts."

A.J. shook his head. "I never saw a girl do that."

"Of course girls—and women—

are magicians," Mrs. Brisbane told him.

"Who is a famous girl magician?" A.J. asked.

Mrs. Brisbane thought for a moment. "I don't know the names of many magicians. There was Houdini, of course. He was a great escape artist a long time ago."

"If Houdini were still alive, what would he be?" Kirk asked.

Before anyone could answer, Kirk said, "The oldest person in the world!"

Everybody laughed except for A.J.

"Houdini was a *man*," he said.

"Maybe Miranda will be the first famous female magician," Mrs. Brisbane told him.

"I'll show you, A.J.," Miranda said.

"YES-YES-YES!" I squeaked.

The bell rang and all my friends went to their tables.

I didn't hear anything about magic for a while, because Mrs. Brisbane sent my friends to the library.

"Take your notebooks," she reminded them as they headed out the door. "You'll want to find out as much as you can about your jobs."

Mrs. Brisbane left with the rest of the class.

When we were alone, I turned toward Og's tank. "I'm really

good at escaping from my cage,"
I said. "Like that magician called
Houdini."

"BOING-BOING!" Og hopped
up and down.

I sighed. "I may be the best
hamster escape artist in the
world, but nobody knows it . . .
except you."

Og dived into the water in his tank and splashed loudly.

I grabbed the notebook and pencil hidden behind my mirror. Quickly, I added something to the list of jobs I could do.

ESCAPE ARTIST

~~~~~

I made sure my notebook was safely back in its place when the class returned to Room 26.

"I think you got a good start," Mrs. Brisbane said. "But don't forget, I want you to come dressed for your job when you present your report on Monday. And bring as many props as you'd like."

Sayeh shyly raised her hand. "Mrs. Brisbane, would it be all right if I used Humphrey for my report?"

"Of course, Sayeh," Mrs. Brisbane said.

"No!" Miranda exclaimed. "I'm planning to use Humphrey! I signed up to take him home for the weekend so we can practice.

I'm sorry, Sayeh, but it's really important."

Sayeh looked VERY-VERY-VERY disappointed.

"Could one of you use Og?" Mrs. Brisbane asked.

Sayeh suddenly looked much happier. "Yes! I'd love to have Og help me."

It was great to see Sayeh smile. Og hopped up and down. "BOING-BOING!" he said.

All afternoon, I wondered how Miranda would use me in her magic act.

Would she pull me out of a hat?

It's dark and stuffy inside a hat.

Would she turn me into a frog?

I think one frog is enough for Room 26. And I like being a hamster!

Would she saw me in half?

Once I saw a magician on TV saw a woman in half. (Luckily, he put her back together again.)

"NO-NO-NO!" I squeaked. "Please don't saw me in half! I'm already really small!"

Some of my classmates began to giggle.

"Humphrey sounds very excited about being in your presentation," Mrs. Brisbane said.

Then I remembered Miranda's terrible dog, Clem. His breath is awful and he hangs around my cage.

And I'm *sure* he doesn't hang

around my cage because he wants to be friends!

Just thinking about Clem makes me shiver and quiver.

"I'm not excited," I shouted. "I'm scared!"

My friends just giggled again, because all they heard was "SQUEAK-SQUEAK-SQUEAK."

~~~~~

Later that night, I took out my little notebook and stared at my list of hamster jobs.

I had a few new ideas. The first one was:

REPORT HELPER

Yes! I am very good at that.

I thought some more about other jobs. Suddenly, I thought about Clem and his very large teeth again.

Clem had a job for me: Dog Toy. Thank goodness that is not a real job!

I didn't add it to my list. But still, I didn't sleep a wink that night.

Not one wink.

Disappearing Act

Of course, I was nervous when I got to Miranda's house on Friday afternoon.

But Clem was nowhere to be seen.

"Humphrey, my mom sent Clem to Gran's house for the

weekend so he wouldn't bother you," Miranda announced.

That made me feel MUCH-MUCH-MUCH better.

"I have a lot of work to do this weekend," Miranda said as she set my cage on her desk. "And I need your help."

"I'm ready!" I squeaked.

"First, I have to look like a magician," Miranda said.

She disappeared into her closet.

When she came out again, she was wearing a black jacket with long sleeves and a tall black hat.

"Ta-da!" she said.

"I'm Magic-Miranda now."

I always call her Golden-Miranda because of her golden hair. But she looked like Magic-Miranda with the hat on.

Miranda pulled a small table covered with a black cloth to the center of her room. There was a big box on the table.

"This is my magic table," she said.

She opened the box and pulled out a wand. "Every magician needs a magic wand."

"Of course," I agreed.

Next, Miranda put the box

on the floor and brought over a stack of books. After she put them around the edge of the table, she opened my cage and gently took me out.

She set me in the middle of the books so I wouldn't fall off.

Then she said, "Humphrey! What have you got in your ear?"

"In my ear?" I squeaked. "Nothing!"

Like all hamsters, I store food in my cheek pouches. But I don't put *anything* in my ears.

She reached one hand toward

my ear. "Why, look!" she said. "It's a dime!"

She held up a small silver coin.

"Eeek!" I squeaked.

It didn't seem possible. Hamsters don't have much use for money.

And my ear is much too small to hold a dime!

Miranda stroked my back with her finger and laughed. "Don't worry, Humphrey," she said. "It wasn't really in your ear. It's a trick."

That made me feel a LOT-LOT-LOT better.

"My uncle Wally used to pull coins out of my ear when I was little," she said. "When I got older, he taught me the trick."

"How do you do it?" I asked.

"I had the coin hidden in my hand the whole time," she said.

She did the trick again. This time, she showed me how she hid the dime between her fingers.

"It takes a lot of practice to learn a magic trick," Miranda explained. "I probably tried this a hundred times."

Wow! That's a lot of practice.

"You can help me with the next trick," she said.

She took out a deck of cards.

She shuffled them several times

and told me, "This is to make sure the cards are all mixed up."

Miranda set the deck of cards in front of me and spread them out facedown. "Pick a card," she said. "Any card."

I moved forward a few steps and sniffed one of the cards. It didn't have much of a smell, so I moved along.

One of the cards smelled a little bit like berries. I don't know why a card would smell like berries. Maybe someone was playing a

card game and eating berries at the same time.

I headed for the berry-smelling card and sniffed some more. Yum!

Miranda picked up that card. She held it so I could see the front but she couldn't. "This is the card you picked. Remember it," she said.

The card had a 6 in one top

corner and an upside-down 6 in a bottom corner. And there were six red hearts in the middle.

"Got it?" Miranda asked.

I squeaked.

She put the six of hearts back with the other cards. "I'll cut the deck," she said.

I watched carefully as Miranda moved sections of the deck around. I tried to figure out where my card went, but the backs of the cards all looked alike.

Then Miranda spread the cards on the table faceup.

A few seconds later, she picked up a card and said, "Here's your card."

It was *my* card—the six of hearts!

How did she do that?

"It's not magic," she said. "There's a secret to it."

I begged her to tell me the secret, but I guess all she heard was SQUEAK-SQUEAK-SQUEAK.

Miranda reached down into the box and pulled out a paper cup.

While she held the cup in one hand, she pulled a small wooden bead out of her box.

"Now I'll show you how to make a bead disappear," she said. "Watch closely."

"I will!" I squeaked.

Miranda dropped the bead into the cup. Then she picked up her

magic   wand
and   waved   it
over the cup.

"Abracadabra,
abracaday. Make the bead go
away," she said.

She set the wand back
on the table and
turned   the   cup
upside down.

But the bead
didn't   tumble

out! Where could it have gone?

"There's no bead in the cup,"
Miranda said. Then she reached

into her pocket.
"Because the
bead is *here*."
She pulled
the bead out of
her pocket.

She really was Magic-Miranda!

"Wow!" I squeaked.

Miranda bowed. "I really shouldn't tell you how I did that," she said. "Magicians are supposed to keep their tricks secret."

I was disappointed until Miranda added, "But since you're

going to be my assistant, I'll tell you."

Oh, it was a clever trick!

First, there were two matching beads. One of them was in her pocket the whole time!

Second, there was a hole in the bottom of the cup, which she had hidden from me. When she dropped the bead into the cup, it fell through the hole and into her hand. When she turned the cup upside down, that bead stayed in her hand.

Then she put her other hand

into her pocket to get the second bead. It looked as if the bead had magically moved.

It was a very tricky trick!

Miranda showed me more tricks.

She made a pencil stick to her hand without anything holding it on!

She made a spoon bend and then brought it back to its shape.

I couldn't figure out how she did those things, and she didn't tell me.

Late in the afternoon, Miranda's

mom came in to see how we were doing.

"Miranda, I hope you haven't worn Humphrey out," she said. "After all, this is his day off from school."

"He's going to be my assistant," Miranda said.

"That's a good idea," her mom said. "But please don't make Humphrey disappear."

Miranda smiled. "I won't. I'm going to make *A.J.* disappear!"

"NO-NO-NO!" I said.

I was pretty sure that Miranda would get in a lot of trouble if she made A.J. disappear.

What would his family think?

Miranda put me back in my cage and set up a new trick.

In front of her was an upside-down glass and a piece of paper made into a tube.

She showed us that the tube was completely open inside.

Next, she held up a photo. "Here's A.J.," she said. "This was taken at his birthday party."

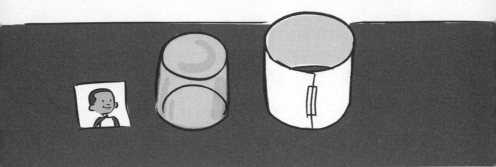

Miranda put the photo on the table. "And now I'm going to make him disappear."

She placed the paper tube over the glass so we couldn't see the glass at all. Then she put the glass on top of the photo so we couldn't see it anymore.

Miranda slid the glass across the table. "Presto-chango."

I still couldn't see the photo because it was under the glass.

She tapped the glass with her magic wand two times.

"And now you'll see . . ." Miranda pulled the paper tube off the glass. "No more A.J."

I could see the glass, but the photo of A.J. was gone!

Miranda's mom clapped her hands. "Wonderful! Now can you bring him back?"

Miranda nodded. She put the paper around the glass and slid it across the table.

"Hocus-pocus!" Miranda said.
She tapped her wand two times
and lifted the glass.

The photo was back!

Miranda was REALLY-REALLY-
REALLY magic!

The Amazing Humphrini

On Sunday, Miranda and I practiced most of the day. She began to include me in the act.

At the beginning of the card trick, she said, "My assistant, the

Amazing Humphrini, will now select a card."

The Amazing Humphrini! That name made me feel like a real magician.

"After you pick the card, I'll show it to the class so they can memorize what it is," she explained.

"Great!" I squeaked.

Then she did the vanishing bead act. Just before she pulled the second bead out of her pocket, she looked at me and said, "Where do you think the bead has gone, Humphrini?"

I squeaked and she said, "You're right! It's in my pocket."

It was HARD-HARD-HARD work, but I knew the class would love Magic-Miranda's act.

Monday morning was extra exciting in Room 26.

It was amazing to see all my friends dressed for different jobs.

A.J. wore his soccer uniform, and Seth wore a white jacket, like a doctor.

Gail had dressed like Mrs. Brisbane, and she had a gray wig on her head.

I couldn't wait to see what

Richie wore, because he'd had so much trouble deciding what he wanted to do when he grew up.

To my surprise, he didn't dress like a police officer, an Olympic runner *or* a chef.

Instead, he wore a suit and tie!

"What are you going to be when you grow up, Richie?" Mrs. Brisbane asked.

"I'm going to be a banker and have piles and piles of money!" he said.

Just before the bell rang, I turned to my neighbor, Og. "Don't worry if Miranda calls me Humphrini," I told him. "That's my magician's name."

"BOING-BOING!" Og yelled, and he hopped up and down.

Mrs. Brisbane began the reports right away.

Stop-Giggling-Gail didn't even giggle once during her report. She explained how teachers like Mrs. Brisbane work hard to make sure that their students learn things that will help them grow and be successful.

A.J. explained how much practice and training went into becoming a soccer star. He also showed some great moves, kicking the ball around the room.

Speak-Up-Sayeh told us that when she grew up, she wanted to be a veterinarian. She would take care of all kinds of animals, from horses to frogs and hamsters!

As always, Sayeh spoke softly. "I would like to be a veterinarian because I love math and science and I love animals," she said. "A vet makes sick animals better and does things to help healthy animals stay healthy."

"Go, Sayeh!" I squeaked.

My friends all laughed.

Then she walked over to Og's cage and told us things she had learned about caring for frogs.

"A frog that jumps a lot is a healthy frog," she said.

Og jumped all around the land side of his tank. "BOING-BOING-BOING-BOING!"

Everyone laughed and so did I.

I was HAPPY-HAPPY-HAPPY to see that Og was healthy.

The reports went on.

I didn't understand everything Richie said when he explained something called *interest* on money, but I found his talk very *interesting*.

Kirk told a lot of funny jokes when he talked about being a comedian.

My favorite joke was when he said, "Did I tell you about the day my brother found carrots growing out of his ears?"

He paused and then said, "He was so surprised! He'd planted radishes!"

When everyone had stopped laughing, Kirk explained that the last part that makes you laugh is called the *punch line*.

Seth told us he wanted to be a doctor for humans. He showed us how to take a pulse and talked about yucky things called germs.

Time flew by, and it was soon time for lunch.

Mrs. Brisbane let Miranda prepare her magic act while everyone was out of the room.

I watched as she carefully set

up a table with the black cloth. She put a toy fence around the edges to protect me.

Miranda made sure that everything she needed was in her box. With her back to Mrs. Brisbane, she carefully put one of the wooden beads in her pocket.

Then she and
Mrs. Brisbane left
to go eat lunch.

"Wait until you see her act,"
I told Og. "She really is Magic-
Miranda!"

Og seemed very excited as he
splashed around in the water.

And then I saw it: the
wooden bead. It was on the
floor, near the leg of the table.

I couldn't believe my eyes!
It must have fallen out of
Miranda's pocket.

She'd be terribly upset when she reached for it and it was gone.

I glanced at the clock. Eeek!

The students would be coming back soon. Miranda's trick would be ruined without the bead. But if I hurried, maybe I could put it on her table without getting caught outside of my cage.

I jiggled my lock-that-doesn't-lock and raced past Og's tank.

"BOING-BOING!" Og said.

"I've got something important to do," I squeaked.

I slid down the leg of the table and headed straight for the bead.

I knew I'd need both paws to get to the top of Miranda's table, so I tucked the bead into my cheek pouch.

It didn't taste very good, I'm sorry to squeak.

Just then, the bell rang. There was no time to climb Miranda's table!

I scurried back to my table

and grabbed the cord hanging down from the blinds. Using all my might, I began to swing on the cord. I went HIGHER-HIGHER-HIGHER until I reached the tabletop.

Then I let go of the cord and landed near Og's tank.

Suddenly, the door to Room 26 opened and my friends rushed into the room.

I dashed into my cage and pulled the door behind me.

76

Luckily, no one saw me outside of my cage.

That was a good thing!

But I still had the bead in my cheek pouch. And I didn't know how I'd give it to Miranda without anyone else noticing.

That was a bad thing!

Miranda had on her black jacket and top hat and began her act.

"I am Magic-Miranda," she said.

My mind was racing as Miranda pulled a coin out of Richie's ear.

"How'd you do that?" he asked as my friends all laughed.

But Miranda didn't tell him.

Then she did the trick where the pencil stuck to her hand. And the trick where she bent the spoon.

(I'll tell you a secret. She didn't really bend it, but it looked as if she did.)

Everyone clapped.

Then she took me out of my cage and put me on the table. "Here is my assistant, the Amazing Humphrini," she said.

Everyone clapped again. But all I could think about was the bead in my cheek pouch.

Magic-Miranda began her card trick. When she spread the cards out and told me to pick one, I did.

She asked everyone to look at the card and remember it.

This time, the card had a picture of a queen and four red diamonds on it. And that's the same card Miranda pulled out after shuffling the cards again.

Even Mrs. Brisbane was impressed with that trick!

I thought she'd do the vanishing bead trick next, but instead, she announced that she would make A.J. disappear.

"I don't believe it," he said.

"You'll see." Miranda took out the photo of A.J., which made everyone laugh.

But my friends weren't laughing when she put the photo under the glass and made *it* disappear. (At least it looked as if it disappeared.)

Everyone clapped. And A.J. looked HAPPY-HAPPY-HAPPY to see that only his picture had disappeared.

Miranda had saved the bead trick for last.

Miranda knew everyone would be surprised when she pulled the bead out of her pocket. But I knew that *Miranda* would be surprised when that bead wasn't there.

She placed one bead in the cup and turned it upside down.

When the bead didn't fall out of the cup, everyone gasped.

Miranda reached into her pocket with her other hand.

I saw the look of horror on her face when she realized the bead wasn't there!

I quickly spit the bead out of my mouth.

It rolled across the table and stopped right in the middle.

At first, the room was silent.

Then everyone began to cheer!

All my friends were clearly amazed.

"How'd she do that?" I heard Heidi ask Gail.

Miranda took a bow and pointed to me. "Thank you, Amazing Humphrini," she said.

When the class was quiet again, Mrs. Brisbane told Miranda she was a wonderful magician. "But I don't think it's a good idea to put a bead in a hamster's mouth," she said.

She was right about that!

"But I didn't!" Miranda explained. "I thought it was in my pocket. Humphrey's trick was true magic."

~~~

At the end of the day, Miranda came over to my cage and thanked me.

"I'll never figure out how you got that bead," she said. "But you really are amazing, Humphrini!"

A.J. rushed up to Miranda. "Those tricks were great," he

said. "Could you teach them to me sometime?"

"Sure," Miranda said. "As long as you don't mind learning magic from a girl."

I was glad when A.J. smiled and said, "I guess I was wrong about girl magicians."

That night, when things were quiet in Room 26, I took out my little notebook and pencil and looked at my list.

JOBS I COULD DO
(Besides Classroom Pet)

FAMILY PET

CHEERING-UP HAMSTER

HAMSTER DETECTIVE

HAMSTER ~~ENTERTAINER~~ STAR

ESCAPE ARTIST

REPORT HELPER

Then I added something new:

HAMSTER MAGICIAN
(The Amazing Humphrini)

"You know what, Og?" I squeaked to my neighbor. "There are a lot of jobs a hamster like me could do."

"BOING-BOING-BOING!" he agreed.

"But I still think being a classroom pet is the very best job of all," I said.

And I knew I was right.